COLORED PENCILS

MW01118427

TABLE OF CONTENTS

STAFF

Design/Layout:
Layla Emmett
Leah Pierce
Kaia Kelleher

Editing:
Jonathan Vandergrift

Ads:
River Roberts
Jerrin Fisher

Short Story/Poetry:
Sunny Brontosaurus

Photo:
Jonah Coldwater
Ben Pierce

Articles:
Yeshe Cooley
Cedar Kayrum

Comics/Jokes:
Will Avellar
Tai Nunez

ISBN 978-1-61720-891-1

A Letter from the Director of Blue Mountain School

One of the best parts about working at Blue Mountain School is witnessing the creative learning that takes place when we make room for students to participate fully in the process. **Colored Pencils** is an example of the kind of project that promotes creativity, enhances group work skills, and encourages student responsibility and empowerment in the learning process. Thank you to Jonathan for providing The Unknowns with this opportunity to create something so unique, with space for all of our students' voices, stories, and drawings from age 3 to 12! It takes skill and patience to keep students focused and learning through the lens of this kind of unpredictable project, but that is what Blue Mountain School's educational model is all about.

In a culture obsessed with getting things done quickly, with moving through each day just so that we can get to the next one, with teaching kids what they need to know so that they can pass a test, Blue Mountain School works to present children and families with a different approach to education and to life. As a Contemplative Progressive school, focused on nurturing the unique human beings that each of our students are, we value the slow but steady educational process over a tangible product like grades and test scores. We build relationships with our students by getting to know them and helping them to learn to know themselves, by allowing them to make choices and learn from their mistakes.

The sign at the entrance to Blue Mountain School—a surprise gift from an anonymous artist—gets the point across succinctly. It says "Slow: Free Range Children." It might be a lot cleaner, faster, and more productive to tell students what we think they need to learn and how they should learn it. Teaching through relationship and experience is a much slower and messier process, but it is one that is rich and fruitful beyond the usual measures. It is Free Range quality, without a doubt.

Thanks again to Jonathan and The Unknowns for publishing an informative and creative magazine!

In gratitude,

Shelly

January

Cedars birthday/New years January 1st
Layla's Birthday January 9th
Martin Luther King jr. day January 21st

Februrary

Mardi gras carnival februrary 12th
Valentines Day Februrary 14th

March

St. patricks day March 17th

April

April fools day April 1st

May

River's birthday may 15th

June

World enviroment day June 5
Fathers day June 16
First Day of summer June 21

July

Independance day July 4
Parent day July 28

August

Friendship day August 4
Women equality day august 26

September

Labor Day September 2
Grandparents day September 8
Step family day September 16
International peace day September 21
First day of Autumn September 22
Talk like a pirate day September 19

October

National childrens day October 8
Sweetest day October 19
Halloween October 31

November

Thanksgiving November

December

Leahs Birthday December 2nd
Yeshes Birthday December 11th
Christmas Eve December 24th
Christmas Day 25th
Kaia's Birthday December 25th
Shelly's birthday December 25th

JOKES

KNOCK, KNOCK
WHO'S THERE?
INTERPTING NUKE
INTERUPTING NUKE WH...
BOOM!

WHY DID THE DRAGON
CROSS THE ROAD?
BECAUSE THE CHICKEN
JOKE WASN'T INVENTED
YET.

KNOCK, KNOCK
WHO'S THERE?
DISINTEGRATING RAY
ZAP

WHY'D THE CHICKEN
CROSS THE ROAD?
WHY?
I DON'T KNOW, I WAS
ASKING YOU

HOW DID THE MAN
MOVE THE MOUNTAIN?
HOW?
HE PUSHED IT

AT LEAST IN PEACE

By Sundari Brontosaurus

Needles poked my cheeks until they bled. I heard something. Water. I ran toward the source of the sound. Thorns, and twigs stabbed my tired, dirty, sore, beat up bleeding legs.

I ran faster through the brush, tripping over fallen logs. My ragged cloth for clothing got caught on a branch, and I tripped onto a log. My cloth ripped. Pain shot through my tired flesh, my weak bones, and my bleeding red cheeks. I was suffering. I was dying.

My heart was pumping fast. I had to get to the water. The arrow in my foot wasn't getting any better. I had to get to the water. I had almost forgotten the taste of the cold wet stuff.

If I was going to die, I had to die in the peace. I was going to drown myself. My vision was getting black. I could make out birds waiting in the trees, watching me. I was getting cold. I had to get to the water. I had to die in the peace.

My condition was bad. I had lived the life of the warrior, and should have known how it would end. I had nothing to die proud of. I wished I could start over.

My eyelids shut.

ACATAMUS

By Sunny Brontosaurus

Acatamus smelled of muddy fur. She tossed her small furry head as she looked up into the night sky. The stars shone brightly. But one seemed to be moving. It seemed to get bigger, and bigger. Acatamus left the porch of her home, and went on her night hunt. Her paws scratched the ancient earth as she moved slyly, hunting for prey. Grey whiskers poked out of the face of the young cat. The silver fur on her shoulders moved up and down as she moved. Her yellow eyes patrolled the night ground, looking for prey. She saw movement in the grass. It was a small rodent, a mouse. Acatamus could tell from experience. Acatamus leaped silently, and brutal teeth flashed in front of the mamal's's eyes.

The mouse scampered fearfully away, surprised of the sudden attack. Acatamus ran after the mouse. Some sixth sense told her the mouse was heading towards the construction sites. They ran into the site. Big tire tracks were stamped into the muddy ground. Acatamus continued after the mouse. Giant claws grasped it. Acatamus's head bowed to the ground, as she hovered over her kill. The scene of death shone in the moonlight.

But then a backhoe started moving. Acatamus's head arose from the motionless piece of flesh, and hissed at the backhoe, only to show bloody fangs. From all what Acatamus knew, the giant machines never moved at the dark of night. She picked up the mouse by

ACATAMUS THE CAT

the scruff of its neck and began home. As she left the site, she noticed the star. It seemed to be bigger. There it shone, in the night sky. Like a little glow in the worlds of darkness, that got bigger, and brighter.

Acatamus went through the grasses, and then she was home. She went to her backyard, where she would conclude her meal. She ate all, and left nothing, except for the bones and the heart. She leapt onto the porch of her loving shelter, and went in the cat door, feeling like a proud lion.

MORE JOKES...

WHY DID THE SPIDER CROSS THE ROAD?

TO GET BACK TO HIS "WEBSITE"!

POEMS

LAST AND FIRST BY QUINLAN
LAST BEACH SWIMMING
LAST PICNICKING
LAST SLIP AND SLIDE
LAST SUMMER CAMP
FIRST JUMPING IN LEAVES CAREFULLY
FIRST JACK O LANTERNS
FIRST ZOMBIE DANCE PARTY
FIRST PUMPKIN THROWING

Last and first by Sunny
Last bare feet
Last shorts
Last short sleeves
Last picnics
Last hot days
First scary haunted
house
First biggest leaf pile
First painting pumpkins
First cold rainy days
First snow

Last and first by Anya
Last flower picking
Last berry picking
Last swimming outside
Last bare feet
First leaves changing
colors
First jumping in leaves
First raking leaves
First pumpkin carving
First pumpkin pie

Last and first by Jameson
Last flowers
Last swimming outdoors
Last bees
Last green leaves
Last of some singing birds
First leaf piling
First warm clothes
First snowflakes
First playing freeze tag at school
First playing soccer

**Last and first by
Gabe**
Last rollercoaster ride
Last Hershey park
Last bare feet
First guy with a scor-
pian head
First trick or treating
First changing leaves
First soccer teams

Last and first by Dylan
Last swimming in the pool
Last playing outside
Last playing in water
Last out door picnic
First colorful leaves
First falling leaves
First jumping in leaf pile
First almost having winter
First hurricane

Ethan Pickford
TOTALLY AWESOME
HEATER
EPIC
REAPER
EPIC
AWESOME
PEACE
EPIC
REAPER

This is the Reaper. He summoned a dragon from the Oblivion plain of existence because a S.W.A.T. team was deployed.

t.a.r. [totally-awesome-robot] is destroying Floyd by command of his function=the destruction of humanity!!!

T.a.r.
Out of this world
T.a.r.
Awesome !
Lucky
Lucky
Youthful
Awesome
Wangler
Epic
Super
Out of this world
Mercenary
Epic
Rudimentary
Out of this world
Bling
Out of this world
T.a.r.!!!!!!!

Gabe
Fun, silly, loving
Brother of Autumn
Lover of family
Fun, silly, loving brother
Vaughan.

This is a picture of the temple and archeologists trying to find gold in the temple. My sister, named Autumn, helped make our robots. We used recycled stuff out of the recycle bin. Our robot is built with cardboard, shoe boxes, cardboard tubes, and old cassette tapes for the hair; we used paper for the arms. The head for our robot named Toastina was made out of our old toaster.

This is Unknown. He lives on the sun. He does not eat or drink.

Gavin Greenburg
Unknown
Unbreakable
Never Nervous
Kind to aliens
Not hot
Often awake
Warrior
Never out of Iiideas

Colored Pencils

Lily Byler

Lisa
Laughing
Incredible
Silly
Aaaaeeekkkk

My robot's name is Lisa. She lies around all day and watches TV. She is very rich, but she inherited it from her father. Her invisible rocket ship maids do all her work. One day, she decided to go to Mississippi, so she rode her rocket ship maids to the capital of Mississippi. After that, she went to the playground. Then, she did some sightseeing and headed home.
The end.

Jameson Shortt
Zelda's Great Adventure in a Volcano
I made a person and he was supposed to sit on my spaceship. The person you see is named Zelda on that ship. Zelda is trying to save the people from falling in a pit of lava and to stop the evil villain. His name is Mordo. Zelda is trying to put Mordo in jail.
ZELDA
Zooms through space like an Eagle
Loves to save the Day for All!

UNDER THE PEAR TREE
By Sunny Brontosaurus

Dusk's last rays of sunshine was a tone of dark yellow. The yellow was heavy in the sky. Clouds with pink bottoms hung still above the horizon. The sun--- a ball of glowing red light that seemed to send out bursts of natural energy during the day, and was now somewhere among this yellow sky of clouds.

Night's first breaths sent chills of wind over this land. The long yellow grass of a valley swayed in this breath, and the breath taking their hopes with them to the stars to come. The few trees were rocking back and forth with the wind, branches rustling their leaves.

Hills sprung up like bumps, their shape was a half sphere. Large pointed rocks called mountains were in the background, slicing the sky with their sharp tips.

Atop the largest hill a creek lay, going all the way up, down, and beyond the hill. The water was restless and clear, making a joyful young sound as it spilled over pebbles and smooth stones, capturing the light colors of the rocks.

Rested also atop the hill was a pear tree. The leaves---a green of dazzling perfection. And of course, the pears. The juicy fruit was sweet and ripe---the tastiest and freshest in all the land. The trunk was a hardy thing, thick, sturdy, and tall. The branches stretched out to all of the directions of the compass, and possibly even more. The branches provided shade, creating stillness and peace. Under this shade was a beast.

The beast was big, and had thick golden fur. The beast was laying down on his stomach, and had an arched back. His legs were muscular, but at the moment, they were relaxed. His tail laid down at his feet, being long and flexible. Claws as sharp as steel were rested. The beast had a mane of dark haired fuzz around his head. In the center of this was the face of a sly feline. His nose, rosy pink sprouting silver cords. Jaw closed, hiding his invisible murderous fangs. Because of these, the beast was a true killer. His red eyes observing, black pupils shifted from side to side watching for foe or prey.

Blue Mountain School
SUMMER CAMP

mystery camp june 17 - 21

Solve mysteries using real detective techniques like finger printing, fiber analysis, interviews, and intelligence analysis.

BMS radio show june 24 - 28

Explore traditional local crafts, music, stories, skills and put on a live old time radio show.

circus camp july 8 - 19

Learn skills like juggling, clowning, costume design and hold a circus for friends and family. Returning circus campers will refine skills worked on last summer and try out new skills, too!

$195 per student per week. 15% discount for additional kids in a family. Ages 3-12.

540.745.4234

bluemountainschool.net

Things you might want to know about our sheriff.

Hi, this is Ben and Jonah. Our class called up the sheriff. We asked him if he could come to our class for an interview. These are the questions we asked him.

Our friend Tai was acting so bad we thought that the sheriff was going to arrest him.... JK, JK!!!

Why did you want to become sheriff?

It didn't start as wanting to be sheriff; I wanted to be a police officer. I became a dispatch officer, then a communication officer, then chief deputy. I worked for 3 sheriffs. I decided to run for sheriff and won. Now I am in his third term.

What kind of education/training did he have?

I started at the bottom and worked my way up. When I was a dispatcher I went to dispatch school. When I was a correctional officer I went to Roanoke and did 20 weeks of training. When I was a road officer I went to road school. There is a lot of training in the law enforcement career.

Have you ever been on a pursuit? What it was like!?

I've been on many pursuits over the years. Usually pursuits start at traffic lights, where people try to out run me. We had one about a year ago that started in Roanoke and it came all the way to Floyd. We called it a running road block.

Have you ever wrecked your cop car?

There were some deer accidents, nothing bad. Nothing that was my fault.

Have you ever been in a gun fight? what it was like!?

I've only been in one gun fight. There was a drug dealer we had been chasing for a while, and then we caught him at a local business and tried to arrest him. The criminal tried to run over some of my police officers with his motor vehicle, so they had to fire at him. He was not killed, in fact he is still in prison today.

How many successful cases have you been involved in?

In the thousands!

What was your most exciting case?

A few years ago we had a man hunt after Steven Branscome. He had shot at a police officer. A few days later he was sighted in Floyd County. We had over 200 troopers looking for him. We ended up catching him in Texas. We tracked him using the telephone system. He is in jail now.

"When something bad happens, we pull together to help our community!"

-Sheriff Zeman

Jokes again...

What do you call an alligator in a vest?

An "in-vest-a-gator"!

What did the father buffalo say to his son when he left?

Bison!
Get it? Bye son, like Bison!!!

Ask Audry!

What do I do when my boyfriend won't talk to me?
-Confused

Dear confused,
Talk to him! Call him, text him, talk to him face to face. Nothing will get better by waiting for him!

How do I get my boyfriend to stop talking to other girls?
-Jealous

Dear Jealous,
It is good to express yourself to him. Try talking to him about how you feel. Use "I" statements and remember to not overreact.

My mom lives in California and I think she hates me because I won't go live with her.
-Hurt and motherless.

Dear hurt and motherless,
I don't think she hates you I think she is kind of hurt and daughterless. You could try to tell her "I would love to be in the sun with you but I have friends here and I don't think I am ready for a big switch like that." Sending her letters and talking to her can go a long way!

I broke up with my boyfriend and I like another boy. I still want to be friends and my friend was dating him. Is it worth it?!
-Worth it?

Dear Worth it?,
About you ex. being friends after a broken heart is tough, but giving him space and being open helps, you can have another friend talk to him for you, but give him space and most likely he would rather be friends more than nothing. About the guy you like, MAKE SURE your friend is okay with it. If she is okay with it keeping her posted is the best thing, because if she is okay with it she won't want to feel left out. Remember not to make it awkward between you guys. If she isn't okay with it then it probably isn't worth it. If she broke up with him then she didn't want to date him, if he broke up with her than she may not be over it. Keep her posted first so she doesn't think it is awkward. If you like this guy, go for it! Talk to her but generally it all depends what is in her head and in your heart.

I really like a guy but I never get to see him! I dream about him but what should I do?
-lost

Dear lost,
It depends if it is a long distance relationship (out of state) or he's just an hour away. If you dream about him and you really like him then don't break up with him. Just talk to him a lot and set up a schedule to see each other, like every Friday or Saturday night. But when you do see each oth try to make it memorable.

What should I do if a boy at school always bullies me and there is no way to stop? Is it because he likes me, or is scared of me, or jealous? What do I do to stop?
-Anonymous

Dear anonymous,
Well don't be mean back. Is he bullying you or is it war? It is absolutely possible that he is jealous or scared, but it is also possible that he is a person who takes pleasure in bullying. Take it to people! Talk to your friends and family, and don't talk to him at any cost! If worst comes to worst tell the teacher, yeah, it sucks to be a tattle, but don't put up with people like that!

If you need anything at all Send a letter to me at bmscoloredpencils@gmail.com or send a letter to blue mountain school @ 470 Christiansburg Pike Floyd , VA 24091. You can send anything from Relationships to where the best chocolate is! Please title your letter like "-Dreams". Your letter may or may not be in the magazine!

Thanks
-Audry

Dotted Lines
by Layla Raine Emmett

This is a dotted line drawing. I was inspired to do this drawing by my art teacher, Lore. She taught us about lines and my favorite line was dotted line.

Audreys Corner

Tips

- Ways to get split ends
.Brushing your hair while its wet
.Braiding your hair while its wet
.Blow drying your hair
.Straightening your hair
.Curling your hair
Avoiding these = avoiding split ends

- Washing your face with hand soap won't help your acne, the hand soap will make the oils come back stronger

- Make sure to wash your makeup off every night, do you don't clog up your pores (use face wash, not hand soap)

- Chocolate gives you acne

- The less products you put in your hair, the less split ends you'll have

- Drinking loads of water stops acne

- You're supposed to drink 6-8 cups of water a day to stay healthy

-You need a full 8 hours of sleep, sometimes more, to be fully rested and feel/look good

- Getting dark circle or bags under your eyes is from lack of sleep

- If you feel good, you look good

- After you shave its good to use lotion or moisturizer, so your legs don't get ashy or dry

. Essential Oil Effects

Lavender- Leaves you feelings calm and relaxed. great before bed.

Lemon- Uplifting and clarifying. Also a good astringent.

Peppermint- Wake you up, refreshing.

Jasmine- Makes you feel confident and pretty. Makes you feel dreamy.

Orange-Uplifting to the soul

Eucalyptus- Good for sinus congestion and the lungs.

. Strawberry Body Scrub
1. Use 3-4 strawberries (thawed out are ok, but fresh are MUCH better). You can even use any fruit if you want
2. Cut each strawberry into 4 pieces
3. Pour a half cup of sea or epsom salt into a medium bowl
4. Pour 1 tablespoon of olive oil into the bowl
5. Mix in the strawberries with a fork, mash the strawberries with a fork or your hands
6. Leave on your body for 10-15 minutes then rinse off
makes your skin soft and look great!

Almond Milk and Honey Face Wash
1. Take 6-8 almonds and grade them with a cheese grader or food processor.
2. Take a small bowl and put 2 table spoons of milk it in.
3. Add a spoon of honey
4.Mix the honey, milk, and almonds
5. Gently rub on face and enjoy!
Makes your face smooth and refreshed

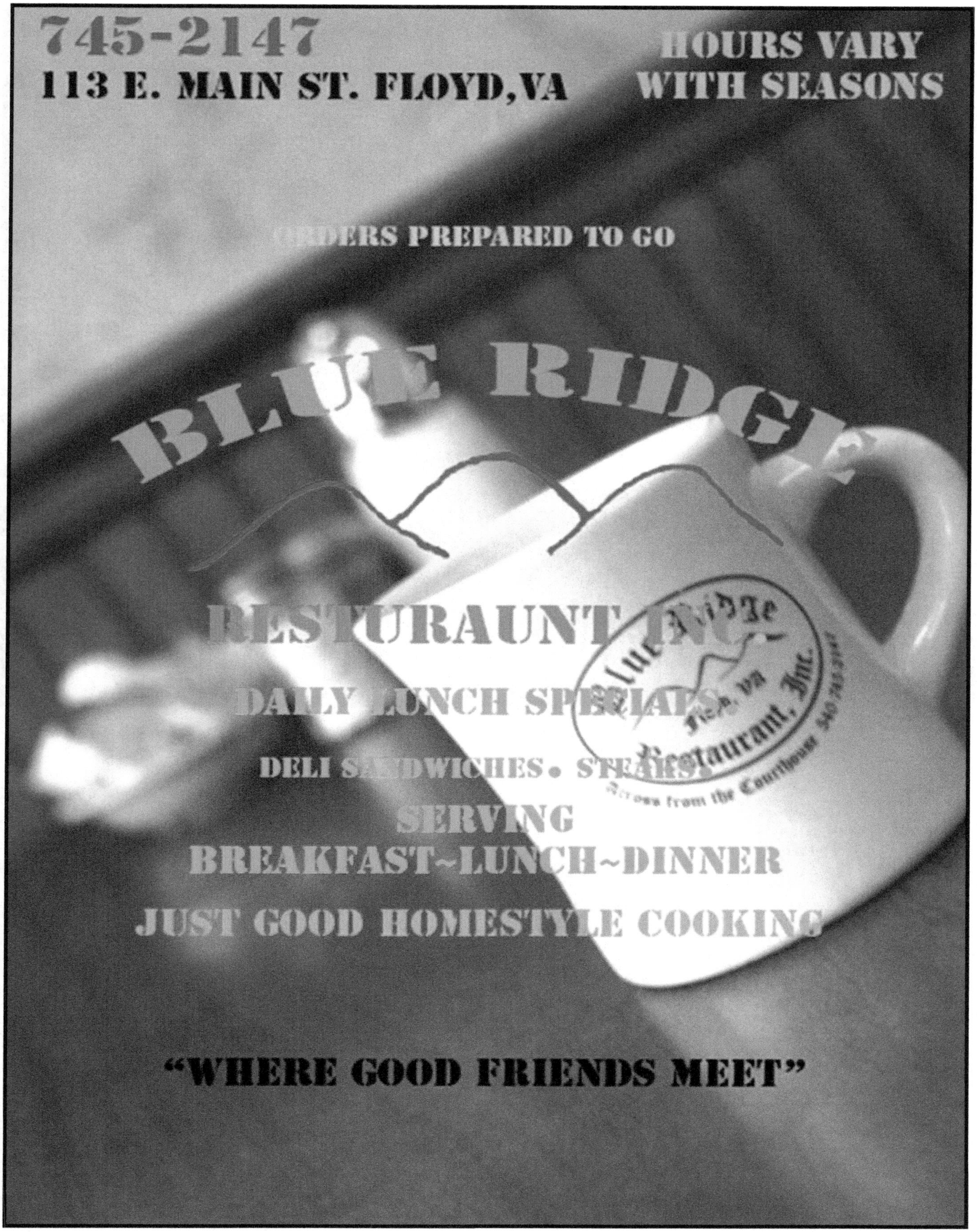
745-2147
113 E. MAIN ST. FLOYD,VA
HOURS VARY WITH SEASONS
ORDERS PREPARED TO GO
BLUE RIDGE
RESTURAUNT INC.
DAILY LUNCH SPECIALS
DELI SANDWICHES • STEAKS
SERVING
BREAKFAST~LUNCH~DINNER
JUST GOOD HOMESTYLE COOKING
"WHERE GOOD FRIENDS MEET"

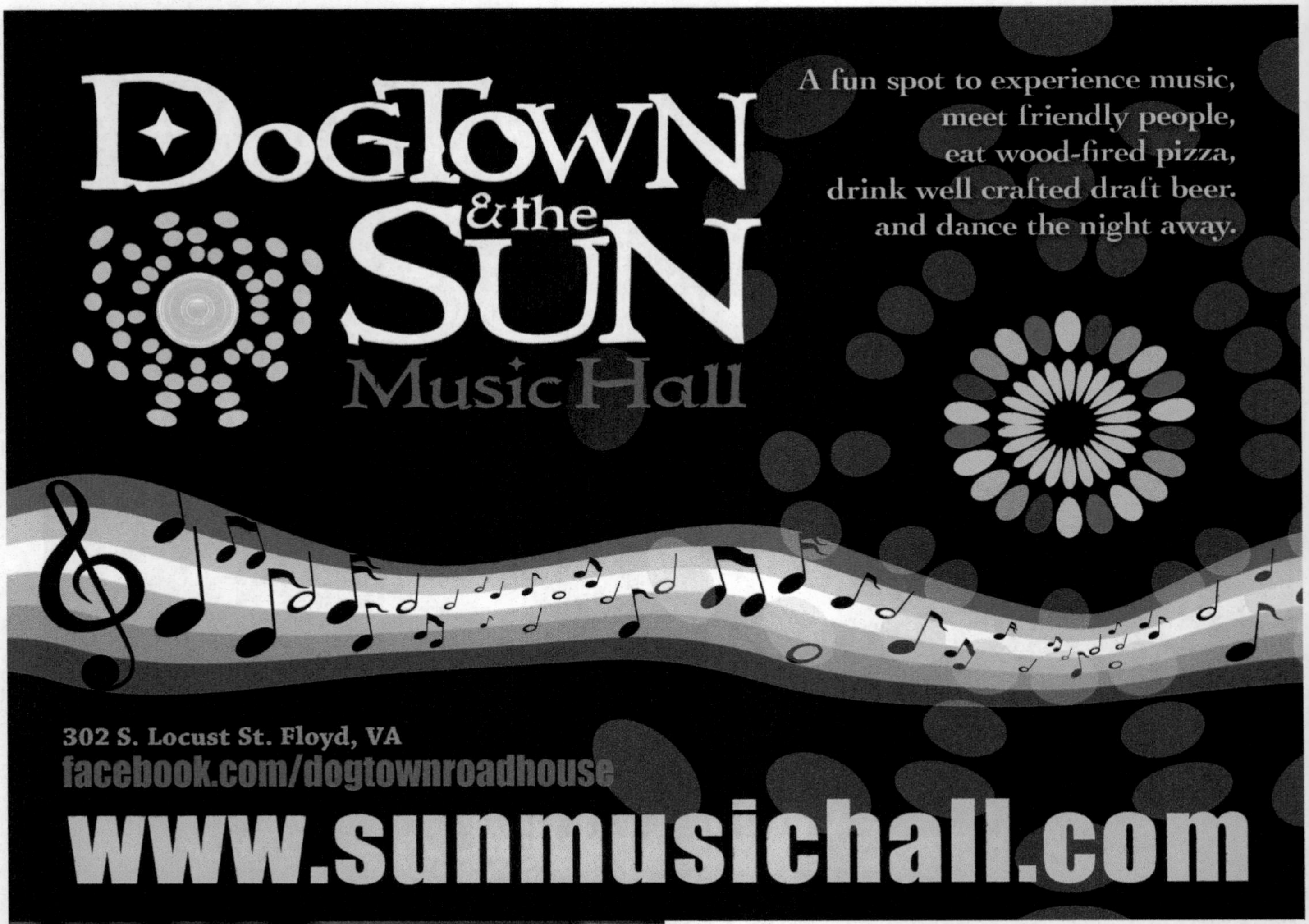
DogTown
& the
SUN
Music Hall
A fun spot to experience music,
meet friendly people,
eat wood-fired pizza,
drink well crafted draft beer.
and dance the night away.
302 S. Locust St. Floyd, VA
facebook.com/dogtownroadhouse
www.sunmusichall.com

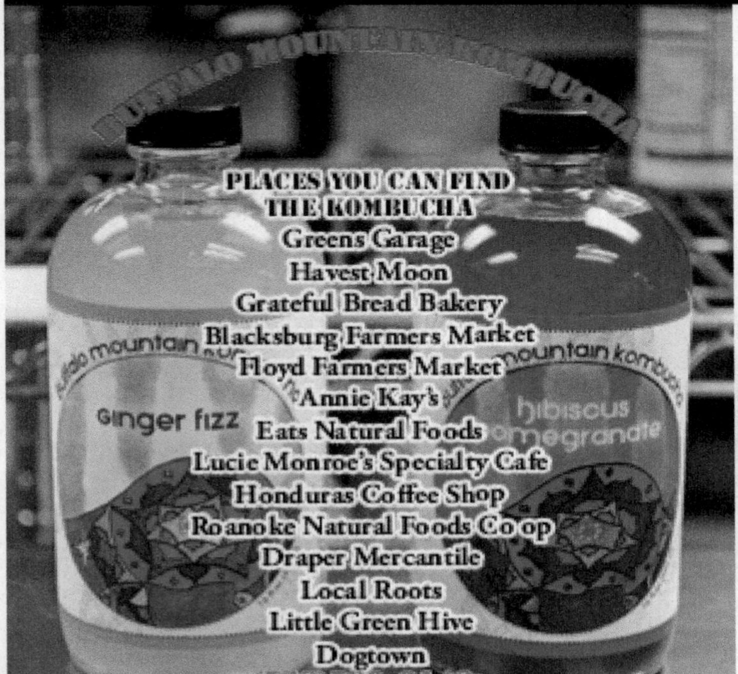
PLACES YOU CAN FIND
THE KOMBUCHA
Greens Garage
Havest Moon
Grateful Bread Bakery
Blacksburg Farmers Market
Floyd Farmers Market
Annie Kay's
Eats Natural Foods
Lucie Monroe's Specialty Cafe
Honduras Coffee Shop
Roanoke Natural Foods Co op
Draper Mercantile
Local Roots
Little Green Hive
Dogtown
ginger fizz
hibiscus
pomegranate

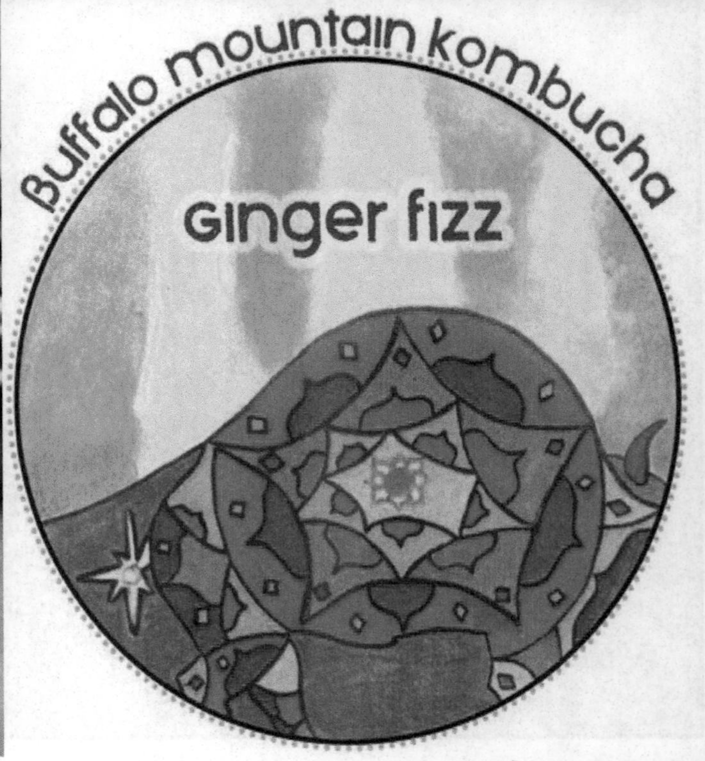
Buffalo mountain kombucha
ginger fizz

BEN AND JONAH'S PUBLIC SERVICE ANNOUNCEMENTS

Don't trip your friends!

Driving is difficult!

Look both ways before crossing the road!

Don't do surgery on your friends!

Colored Pencils

Artemis The Goat
By Tai Nunez and Cedar Kayrum

Day One:

"Hi my name is Artemis. I am no ordinary goat. I am........
……...A spy."

That day I woke up and decided what to eat. There was a moldy shoe half buried in the dirt. I thought for a minute then ran over and shoved it in my mouth. For a second Tai whose two years old, mistook me for a chipmunk that was storing food in his cheeks. Then Tai ran at me, what was he doing? He watched with growing fear, closer, and closer and then Tai sat on me. I was struggling. Then splat I was a pancake.

An hour later I woke up, there were spots before my eyes. Then I got a text message on my phone.
(text message conversation)

Gippy: Hey

Artemis: Hey dude whats up?

Gippy: I am chasing cedar!

Artemis: Sweet!

Gippy: I know right!

Artemis: Watch I am sending cedar on her way.

Gippy: NO.....NO! She's heading for my trof! And there she goes all in the good stuff!
Artemis: I better go.

(New text message)

Commander Jersey: Bailout Artemis. Act normal......
……...They're coming!

Artemis: Yes sir! Can you bump me up to rank Tomato?

Day Two:

"Hi, I am Artemis. I am no ordinary goat…wait, wait I already told you that didn't I, or is it the other way around? Well on with the story."

One night I was dreaming I was getting lifted up by Dorito dude. He was putting me on that thing I think it's called a train, but anyway I fell off and then he started teasing me with cake.

Anyway, I woke up sweaty. There was a moldy cake in the corner of the barn, it looked good. I went over to it. I dragged it over to the middle of the stall. One bite and I would be better. I lowered my mouth then I said…

"GIBBY WHAT ARE YOU DOING HERE?!!!!!!" Then, I looked down the cake was gone! "What's your problem Gibby? That was my 5:00 meal!!!"

Uh oh here comes Tai and Cedar and some of their friends.

One of their friends named Layla said "Let's play princess!"

"And knights!" said the boy they call Jonah.

"I call that one." says Layla.
Oh no, Layla was

pointing at me! And then she sat on me and started saying giddy up , goaty! Down I went.

"Pathetic goat", said Layla.

"I want a turn", said Jonah.

Two hours later:

"Time for a nice tomato", I said to myself. ***Beep*** I got a text. I pull out my iphone. It was from Gibby and it said "May I join you?"

"No you may not!", I replied.

"Uh oh", said Gibby. He had already taken more than my share. I looked down, the tomato was gone.

"NOOOOOOO!!!!!", I screamed.

JOKES, ONE MORE TIME...

WHAT ARE PREHISTORIC MONSTERS CALLED WHEN THEY SLEEP?

A "DINOSNORE"!

WHAT IS THE FRUITIEST LESSON?

HISTORY, BECAUSE IT'S FULL OF DATES!

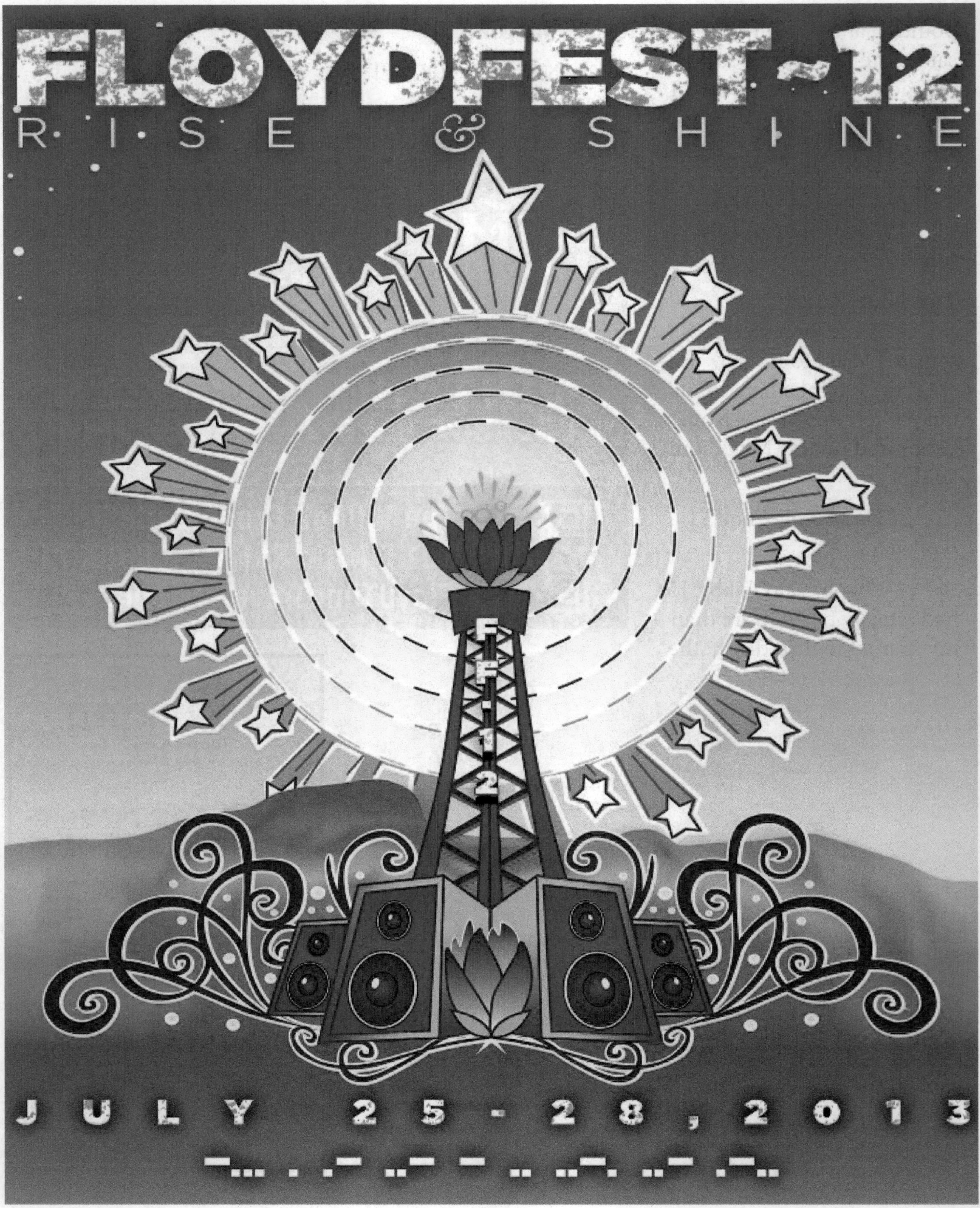

FLOYDFEST~12
RISE & SHINE
FF-12
JULY 25-28, 2013

COMICS

Colored Pencils   23

COLORED PENCILS
Contests!!!

Photography contest rules:

1 .You may only send in 1 photo per person.
2. The photo must be sent in electronically to this email: *bmscoloredpencils@gmail.com*
3. No gross photos aloud in this contest.
4. You must be 15 years old or younger to enter this contest.
5. When submitting a photo you must say your age name and where ever photo was taken.
6. HAVE FUN!!!

SHORT-STORY CONTEST:

Enter your creative writing into Colored Pencil's Short-Story Contest, and the winner's story will be published for the public!

Rules:

1. Must send story to *bmscoloredpencils@gmail.com*
2. A story longer than two pages long will excluded from the contest, for Colored Pencils has limited amount of space
3. Writers are only included if between the ages of six and twenty
4. Only one story will be accepted at a time
5. The winning author's photo will be copied into the magazine along with a free copy of BMS's latest edition of the magazine!

POETRY CONTEST:

Enter your creative writing into Colored Pencil's Poetry Contest, and the winner's poem will be published for the public!

Rules:

1. Must send poem to *bmscoloredpencils@gmail.com*
2. A poem longer than a page long will be excluded from the contest, for Colored Pencils has a limited amount of space
3. Writers are only included if between the ages of six and twenty
4. Only one poem will be accepted at a time
5. The winning author's photo will be copied into Colored Pencils along with a free copy of BMS's latest edition of the magazine!

Colored Pencils

CPSIA information can be obtained
at www.ICGtesting.com
Printed in the USA
LVOW05s0838240916
505968LV00007B/79/P